The Sweet Touch

Lorna Balian

ABINGDON PRESS

Nashville and New York

Library of Congress Cataloging in Publication Data

Balian, Lorna.
    The sweet touch.

    SUMMARY: The genie Peggy's plastic ring conjures up is
only a beginner who doesn't know how to put a stop to the one
wish he can grant.
    (1. Magic—Fiction)   I. Title.
            PZ7.B1978Sw   (E)   74-34217

                ISBN O-687-40773-7

for Peggy and Penny . . . . . .

Peggy found a penny.
She put the penny into a nearby gum machine,
but instead of a gum ball
a shiny, genuine plastic gold ring
rolled into her hand.

Peggy liked the ring well enough,
but she was very fond of sweets
and would have preferred a cherry gum ball.

She put the ring on her finger
and wandered off
hoping to find another penny.

When Peggy was tucked into bed for the night,
she remembered
the shiny, genuine plastic gold ring.
She turned it around on her finger
and rubbed it—
to see if the shiny would come off . . .

. . . the BED TREMBLED,
and out of a puff of smelly dust
a strange, tiny creature appeared.

Peggy yanked the quilt over her head
and huddled with her eyes scrunched shut
and her heart pounding.

"Silly girl," a wee voice whispered
in her ear. "I won't hurt you."

Peggy peeked at him.
"Who are you?" she asked timidly.
"I am Oliver The Magnificent Magic Genie."

He looked so funny and sounded so funny
that Peggy started to giggle.
Oliver was indignant!
He said he had come to grant her one magic wish,
and he certainly wasn't going to do it
if she was going to laugh at him.

Peggy stopped giggling
and looked at Oliver doubtfully.
"If you are a really-truly magic genie
why can't I have three magic wishes
like everybody else?"
Oliver said, "I am only a tiny genie
and rather new at the magic business.
I can only manage one wish."

Well, one wish is better than none,
but it's a difficult thing to decide.
So they sat down to think it over.

Peggy thought it would be lovely
if she could have a big chunk
of creamy chocolate fudge.

Oliver said, "Peppermint sticks might be better.
Red spots pop out
all over me whenever I eat chocolate."

Peggy thought a barrel of gumdrops would be nice.
"A truckload of candied cherries
would be even better!"

"A lollipop tree?"

"Gallons and gallons of root beer!"

"Five hundred ice-cream cones, all flavors!"

"A million jelly beans?"

"Wait!" said Oliver,
"I know just what to do.
I'll give you the MAGIC TOUCH!"
He explained to Peggy that it was not
easy to do, but if he could manage it,
everything she touched would turn into
something sweet.

Peggy agreed that it would be the best way
to get everything they wanted with just
one wish, so she said,

"I WISH THAT EVERYTHING I TOUCH WOULD TURN INTO SOMETHING SWEET!"

Oliver stood on his head and rubbed his wings together.

He wiggled his toes, licked his fingers, and jumped up and down six times.

He whispered some magic words into his pocket,
flew around Peggy's head seventy-three times,
and sat down to say the alphabet backwards.

Suddenly they were surrounded
by the sweet smell of chocolate.
"I've done it! I've done it!" whooped Oliver.
"Your feet! Look at your feet!"

The rug under Peggy's feet had turned to
soft, gooey chocolate,
and it was squishing up between her toes!

Peggy happily licked her toes.
"Touch something else," Oliver begged.
"You know I can't eat chocolate."

Peggy plopped around her room
leaving a gooey chocolate trail
and touching everything in sight.

Her jump rope became a licorice whip.

The bedposts turned to gingerbread.

Her new crayons became candy sticks.
Marbles turned into jawbreakers and bubble-gum balls.
And her very best beads became a necklace of jelly beans.

They nibbled and giggled and ate and ate.

Peggy jumped on the bed
and sank into a very soft marshmallow mattress.

Her pillowcase changed to fine spun sugar,
which quickly tore, and—
feathers billowed out as cotton candy.

"My quilt has turned to taffy, Oliver!" shrieked Peggy. "Help me pull it!"

Peggy took one corner of the quilt,
Oliver took another,
and they pulled and tugged
and twisted the tacky stuff
until they were so tangled up
they could barely move.

"Oliver, I have a tummy-ache," said Peggy.
"I think you'd better turn the wish off now."
"I haven't learned how to do that yet.
I only know how to turn a wish on," said Oliver sadly.

"I'm tired and thirsty," wailed Peggy,
syrupy tears rolling down her face.
"Me too," said Oliver, "and I want to go home,
but I can't fly with all this taffy on my wings."

"What are we going to do?" Peggy asked him.
"Well—let me think about it," said Oliver.

And he thought . . .

and he thought . . .

and he thought . . .
and he thought . . . .

and he thought .

They were both sound asleep
when Oliver's mother flitted into the room.
She had been looking for Oliver all night!

"My, my! What a MESS!" she muttered softly.
"What am I going to do with that boy?"

She pried him loose from the tangle of taffy and scraped the marshmallow from his bottom.

She propped him up and wiggled him until he sleepily muttered the alphabet— frontwards.

She dangled him by the gummy seat of his pants and whirled him around Peggy's head thirty-seven times.

She emptied the magic words out of his pocket.

She jumped down and up with him six times.

She cleaned off his fingers
with the hem of her petticoat
and untangled his sticky wings.

She turned him over her knees,
gave him a love-pat on the fanny,

a kiss on the nose,

and carried him off into the sunrise.

Peggy woke up with her quilt all twisted and tangled about her
and feathers stuck in her hair.

She looked at the shiny, genuine plastic gold ring on her finger
and wondered if the shiny would come off
if she rubbed on it . . .